Paddington
Goes to the Sales

Michael Bond

CARNIVAL

Paddington was woken up on his first morning at thirty-two Windsor Gardens by Mrs. Bird, the Browns' housekeeper, coming into his bedroom carrying a breakfast tray.

He eyed the tray hungrily. It was full of good things. There was grapefruit, bacon and eggs, toast, and a whole pot of marmalade, not to mention a large cup of tea.

"Don't be too long," said Mrs. Bird. "Mrs. Brown is taking you and Judy on a shopping expedition this morning."

Paddington had never had breakfast in bed before, and he soon found it wasn't quite as easy as it looked.

In the end, he decided it would be much simpler if he mixed everything together on one plate and sat on the tray to eat it.

"Oh, Paddington!" exclaimed Judy, when she entered the room a few minutes later. "Whatever's going on? Do hurry up! We're waiting for you downstairs."

Paddington looked up, his face all eggy whiskers and toastcrumbs. He tried to reply, but all he could manage was a muffled grunting noise which sounded like IMJUSTCOMING all rolled into one.

"Really!" said Judy. "You're the stickiest bear imaginable. We're going to Barkridges and if you don't hurry up all the nice things will be gone."

As soon as Judy had left, Paddington gulped down his toast and marmalade. Then, because he didn't believe in wasting things, he packed the remains of the breakfast into his suitcase.

Shortly afterwards, he disappeared into the bathroom in order to have a quick wash.

"That's what I call a *lick and a promise*," said Mrs. Bird, as she waved goodbye at the front door. "And more *promise* than *lick*, if you ask me!"

But Paddington had other things on his mind.

As they made their way up the road, a passing dog let out a loud howl and came running after them.

It was soon joined by several others, and by the time they reached the safety of the Underground station it was rather like the opening night at a dog show.

"If I were you," said Judy, "I'd be more careful when I pack my case in future!"

"I thought I could smell bacon," said Mrs. Brown. "No wonder we were chased."

Paddington had never been shopping in London before and he was most impressed when he saw Barkridges.

It was much bigger than he had ever imagined.

When they were inside the shop, Mrs. Brown led the way to the gentlemen's outfitting department.

"We would like to see some bears' pyjamas, please," she said to one of the assistants.

"Bear's pyjamas?" repeated the man haughtily. "Has modom tried the bargain basement?"

"Certainly not!" said Mrs. Brown. "I've never heard of such a thing! Have you, Paddington?"

"*Never*," said Paddington hotly, and he gave the man one of his special hard stares.

"He's been sleeping in his duffle coat," explained Mrs. Brown, "and we don't want that."

"We certainly don't," agreed the salesman quickly. "Would the young, er . . . gentleman care for something in stripes? They're very popular just now."

"I'd sooner have something with spots, please," said Paddington, pointing to some with flowers spotted all over them. "If I had a pair like those I don't think I'd ever get lost, not even if I fell out of bed by mistake."

"Perhaps you'd like to try them on?" suggested the salesman.

Paddington needed no second bidding.

"The changing rooms are on the right," called the man. But he was too late. Paddington was already too far away to hear.

"I hope they fit," said Judy.

"So do I," agreed the salesman, gazing gloomily at the piles of unsold pyjamas everywhere.

It was "Pyjama Week" at Barkridges, and so far it had been little short of a disaster. No-one seemed to want to buy any, particularly in the style Paddington had chosen, and he had a nasty feeling that if something didn't happen soon they would have an awful lot left on their hands.

However, if Barkridges were unhappy about their pyjamas Paddington was beginning to feel even more unhappy about their changing rooms. They all appeared to be locked.

But at long last he came to a door at the end of the corridor which seemed less tightly shut than the rest and he gave it a push.

Paddington wasn't sure what happened next. As he entered the room there was a noise like thunder and he suddenly found himself lying on the floor surrounded by pots and pans.

At first he thought he must have gone into the wrong department by mistake, and then he caught sight of a screen and a mirror in a corner of the room.

Paddington went behind the screen to change. It didn't take him very long and as he peered at his reflection in the mirror he decided he liked his new pyjamas very much indeed.

Barkridges seemed to have thought of everything for there was even a bed for testing them in, so he climbed in between the sheets and closed his eyes.

Paddington was just about to fall asleep when he heard a rather strange noise. At first, he thought it came from under the bed

It sounded rather like rain.

He sat up, and nearly fell out of bed with surprise at the sight which met his gaze.

There, on the other side of an
enormous sheet of glass, was a sea of
faces.

It wasn't rain he could hear at all.
It was people clapping.

"And what," said a man standing at the foot of the bed, "are you doing in our shop window, bear?"

"Your shop window?" repeated Paddington in surprise. "I thought it was a changing room."

He suddenly wished he hadn't chosen such unusual pyjamas, for he had a nasty feeling he'd been spotted in more ways than one.

As he climbed out of bed a loud cheer came from the pavement outside.

Paddington gave a bow and raised his hat several times. Then he turned  to the man. He had a feeling he was in trouble again.

"I'm afraid," he announced, "I must have taken the wrong turning by mistake."

But, to his surprise, the man wasn't at all cross. In fact he even offered to help tidy up.

And in no time at all Barkridge's window was as good as new.

"You see," said the man, "since people saw you wearing our pyjamas they all want some. They've been selling like hot cakes. You're what we in the trade call a 'trend setter'.

"Look at them . . .

". . . they've all gone."

The manager placed his hand on Paddington's shoulder.

"Barkridges," he said, "is grateful. If there is anything you would like as a present . . ."

Paddington's eyes gleamed. All the excitement had made him feel hungry, and he thought of asking for one of the hot cakes the manager had mentioned.

Then he caught sight of the very thing he wanted.

"I'd like some of those Wellington boots, please," he announced.

"Wellington boots it shall be!" said the manager. He beckoned to an assistant who rushed forward with a selection of pairs.

Paddington tested them carefully one by one until he found a pair to his liking.

"They'll be very useful if it ever rains when I'm in bed," he exclaimed. "It'll stop the ends of my pyjamas going soggy. I wouldn't want that to happen, especially now you haven't got any more left."

This story comes from MORE ABOUT PADDINGTON
and is based on the television film. It has
been specially written by Michael Bond
for younger children.

Carnival
An imprint of the Children's Division
of the Collins Publishing Group
8 Grafton Street, London W1X 3LA

Published by Carnival 1988
Reprinted 1989

ISBN 0 00 194451 9

Printed & bound in Great Britain by
PURNELL BOOK PRODUCTION LIMITED
A MEMBER OF BPCC plc